CAT RINE and **LAURENCE ANHOLT** are an award-winning
hu nd-and-wife team who have worked together on more than
2 picture books, published all over the world in more than
30 diff languages. Their books have won numerous awards and been
featured o io and television. *Chimp and Zee* was winner of the prestigious
Gold tlé Award. Their latest picture book for Frances Lincoln is
One Wor gether. Laurence is also the author of *Stone Girl, Bone Girl,*
wit eila Moxley, and *Seven for a Secret* and *Two Nests* with
James Co one. He also wrote and illustrated the internationally bestselling
Anholt's ts series about great artists and the children who knew them.
Laurence and Catherine live in Devon.

Discover about Catherine and Laurence Anholt at www.anholt.co.uk

red

green

brown

orange

black

goat

gorilla

goose

mole

mouse

moose

sheep

seal

snail

A huge enormous whale.

 Which animal would be a good pet?

Those naughty twins are painting everything...

yellow yard

orange coat

pink palm

purple boat

green garden

blue bed

...ld Mumkey painted red.

...her colours can you see? ☆

Whatever the weather,
Chimp and Zee play outside...

windy

wet

warm

sun

snow

storm

freezing, foggy frost.
Chimp and Zee are lost.

 What's the weather like today?

Chimp and Zee are busy every day.

Monday - monkeying about at the market

Tuesday - tidying toys in the treehouse

Wednesday - whizzing about in the wind

Thursday - talking on the telephone

Friday–finding frogs with friends

Saturday–squelching through the slimy swamp

And... Sunday is FUN DAY!

 What do YOU do every day?

Chimp and Zee are learning to count...

1 mouse in a house

2 twins on swings

3 goats in boats

4 foxes in boxes

5 kittens in mittens

6 owls with towels

7 moles in holes

8 rats in hats

9 bugs on rugs

10 sheep asleep

Can you count too?

It's bathtime
for Chimp and Zee.

Chimp and Zee are in the bath playing with the bubbles —
bubbly nose and bubbly toes
and great big bubbly puddles.

 boat

 mirror

 comb

 plug

 soap

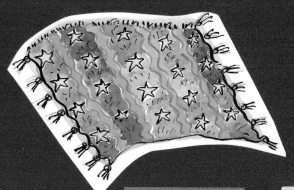 towel

 toothbrush

 mu

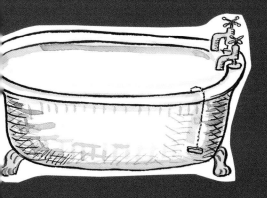 bath

 duck

 chair

sham

 Are YOU a monkey at bathtime too?

Chimp and Zee are going to bed.

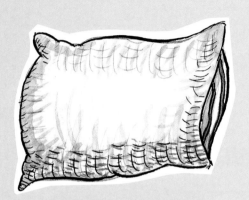

pillow

picture-book

pyjamas

bear

bed

bananas

mobile

milk

moon

Hope to see you soon.

Goodnight Chimp and Zee.

red

green

brown

orange

black

purple

yellow

white

blue

pink

MORE PICTURE BOOKS BY CATHERINE AND LAURENCE ANHOLT
FROM FRANCES LINCOLN CHILDREN'S BOOKS

ONE WORLD TOGETHER
978-1-84780-405-1

I want a friend but who will I choose?
Take a trip around the world, meet children from lots of different places and peep into their lives. This is a delightful story about friendship across nations and cultures, in which one small child visits nine different countries to find a friend – and ends up being friends with ALL the children he meets. Includes a fabulous pull-out world globe.

"A brilliant book to make finding new friends seem fun and exciting, with wonderful diversity and inclusion."
Rhino Reads

Discover all the *Chimp and Zee* books

"Imbued with a joyful energy, making this a bouncy daytime read" –
The Ultimate First Book Guide

ISBN 978-1-84507-932-1   ISBN 978-1-84507-069-4   ISBN 978-1-84507-597-2

Frances Lincoln titles are available from all good bookshops.
You can also buy books and find out more about your favourite titles,
authors and illustrators on our website: www.franceslincoln.com